THE PIRATE'S EYE

written & illustrated by ROBERT PRIEST

HOUGHTON MIFFLIN COMPANY BOSTON 2005

For my wife, Elisa

Special thanks to my friend Jack

Copyright © 2005 by Robert Priest

www.houghtonmifflinbooks.com

The text of this book is set in 15-point Californian.
The illustrations are airbrushed enamel on clayboard.

Library of Congress Cataloging-in-Publication Data
Priest, Robert (Robert H.)
The pirate's eye / by Robert Priest.
p. cm.
Summary: When Captain Black the pirate loses his glass eye, a pauper finds it
and draws the images of the captain's life that he sees within it.
ISBN 0-618-43990-0
[1. Pirates—Fiction. 2. Drawing—Fiction.] I. Title.
PZ7.P93429Pi 2005   [E]—dc22   2004013200

ISBN 13: 9780-618-43990-4

Manufactured in China
SCP 10 9 8 7 6 5 4 3 2 1

ONE WINDLESS MORNING, just south of the Sargasso Sea, two pirate ships were locked in a friendly skirmish.

On deck, the pirates were engaged in their favorite pastime, wheeling and stealing. In the course of doing what only comes naturally to a pirate, a certain Captain Black got a little too close to the tip of a rival's sword, and out popped his piratey glass eye!

This may have deterred another pirate, but not Captain Black. Without missing a step, he continued to parry. His eye fell to the slippery deck and came to rest behind a coil of rope.

Later that afternoon, with the battle won and its hold full of gold, the captain's ship docked in port. When the weathered old vessel bumped the pier, the pirate's eye rolled off the deck and bounced into town.

Captain Black, napping after the battle, awoke with the bump. Realizing his eye was missing, he rushed up to the deck to find it. He searched the poop deck, scoured the upper deck, and combed the lower deck. He queried the first mate, questioned the second mate, and examined the third mate. Nowhere was his eye to be found.

"I shall not rest," he cried, "until I find my precious eye!"

Not far away, the glass eye rolled along, eventually coming to rest among a group of children playing marbles.

Without batting an eye, the children played with the errant orb.

Then they got up and left, leaving the oddball eyeball behind. It spent the night in the road, under the stars.

The next morning was clear and sunny when a pauper named Sandpiper came strolling along. He noticed the shiny round object in the road. Picking it up, he added it to the collection of bric-a-brac in his coat pocket.

Later, in his rickety shack, Sandpiper emptied the contents of his pockets onto the kitchen table. Spreading everything out, he looked at each object carefully.

"Hmmm, this is unusual," he said, holding up the glass eye.

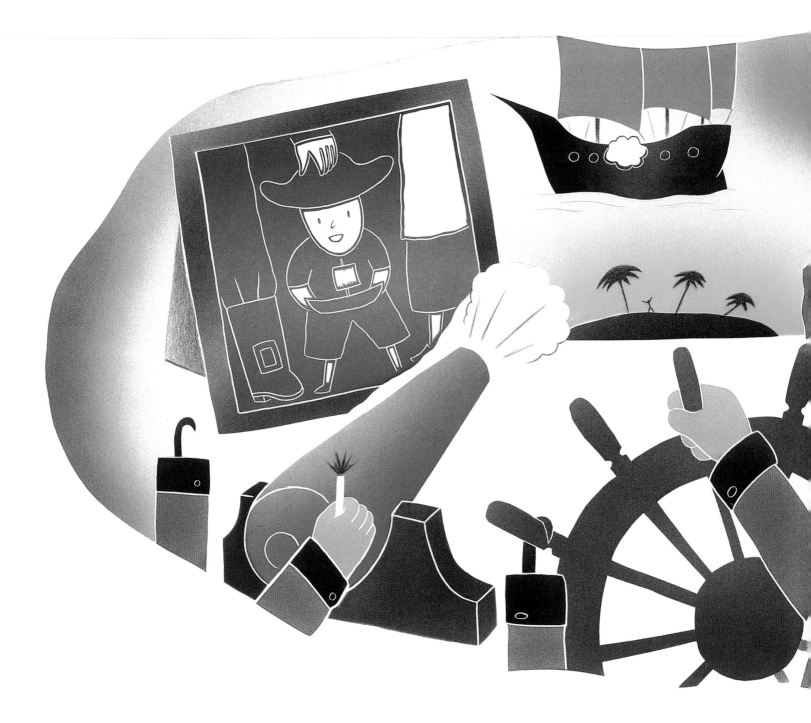

He peered at it closely, and, like a sorcerer's crystal ball, images swirled and floated within the small glass sphere. These images told the story of a strange and interesting life, the life of a seafaring pirate.

In the glass eye, Sandpiper saw scenes of the pirate as a child and scenes of the pirate as a man, scenes of mischievous boyhood and scenes of crime and treason!

Meanwhile, the bedeviled Captain Black journeyed in search of his missing eye. Wherever he sailed he sought clues to its whereabouts. Unsettled and confused, the pirate was lost without his magical lens. "That eye has been with me through gale and through hail, through high tide and low. By hook or by crook, *I must find it!*"

Sandpiper journeyed too, illustrating each adventure that floated to the surface of the glass eye. One day the eye went dark and the story was completed. He fittingly titled his book *A Pirate's Life*. Taking the eye from its stand, he hung it around his neck with a string. Then he made a copy of his book, wrapped it in gift-wrapping, and gave it to his friend Francis, the grocer. He gathered the village children together and gave them books as well, reading his book to the little ones who were too young to read.

Sandpiper put more copies of his book in a cart and pushed it along the sandy roads. He gave a book to the twins who owned the bakery and often gave him a loaf of bread when he couldn't buy one. He gave a book to the old woman who often hired him for an odd job when he couldn't find one.

And he gave a book to the fisherman who sometimes brought Sandpiper a fish when he couldn't catch one.

Sandpiper gave copies of his book to *all* the surprised villagers he met along the way, to all the generous people who had been kind and caring to him over the years.

Meanwhile, up the coast a ways, in a nearby town, Captain Black was at the local public library checking the Lost and Found for his missing eye. It was then that he noticed something odd on a nearby shelf. Upon closer inspection he realized he was looking at something familiar — *his own face*, on a book, *about his own life*!

"Blow me down!" he cried.

"Shhhhhhh," the librarian hushed.

"How can this be?" growled the pirate. "And how long will it be before they have me in shackles? Who dares tell the story of *this* pirate's life!"

In a stormy rage he commandeered a ship and sailed up and down the coast. After asking a few questions, he found the pauper's rickety shack by the dunes. He pounded on the door — *Bang, Bang, Bang.* "Come out, you scoundrel," he bellowed.

Slowly the door opened, and out stepped Sandpiper.

"Pirate," he said. "It's you!"

"Aye, I imagine it is, pauper. And how, pray tell, do you know *all* about *this* pirate's life?"

"Through this, sir," said Sandpiper, handing Captain Black his eye.

Astonished, the pirate quickly placed his long-lost eye where it had once rested. Images began to swirl and float as they once had, but now, instead of seeing *his* life, he saw the life of Sandpiper.

He saw scenes of struggle and hardship. He saw scenes of generosity and kindness, the kindness of the townspeople toward Sandpiper and Sandpiper's kindness toward them.

Captain Black's face softened and his shoulders slumped. For once he had seen another man's life through his very own eye, and he felt ashamed of his wildness, his robbery, and his hysteria.

Quickly he drew his sword ... and flung it into the salty sea.

"That be it for me, matey," he said. "My life will be different from this day forward. There will be no more pirating the seas for me."

Well, despite his promise, nothing can keep a pirate from the seas, and soon Captain Black was back upon the waves, but this time as a peaceful merchant seaman.

And nothing could keep Sandpiper from his drawings and his books.

When Captain Black returns to the village after a voyage, he is always greeted on the pier by Sandpiper. Often the two friends will gather the children of the village together and tell them a story or two. Then, if there's time, they'll tell them the best story of all—the one about the *pirate's eye*.